Walker Drive
A Paranormal Diary

Nicholas Irving

CONTENTS

ACKNOWLEDGMENTS

To my younger self, still in grade school. The one that
decided to write a scary book with his best friend,
Dre…It's been an unforgettable time, getting a chance to
reconnect and do this again.

ACKNOWLEDGMENT

WHY

I was in grade school

when I first decided to sit down and type a book. I wasn't sure what the book would be about, other than I wanted to tell a story. So, it took some time to sort out a few ideas before finally settling on one in particular.

One of my favorite books I loved to read and have read was the Goose Bumps novel series. The series, by R.L Stine, would later become a television series on the children's program Nickelodeon and a movie. These popular 90s novels were a collection of horror stories for young readers. The books usually carried the same theme, involving children in scary situations in a paranormal world. And, in the end, the kid triumphs over the evil.

Inspired by the Stine series, I decided to tell a scary story of my own. Having a rough start initially, I enlisted the help of my childhood best friend, Andre. I always saw Andre, *Dre* is what we called him, as being smarter than I was. Receiving a straight-A report for him was nothing to brag about or new to him. School, at times, seemed too easy to him and far from a challenge.

Every day after school, Dre and I sat behind my dad's computer and typed. Some days, we'd work all weekend and skip out on playing outdoors. Whether Dre wanted to help or not, I couldn't distinguish between the two.

He disregarded the long hours, a neverending plot, and my make-it-up-as-you-go approach. No matter what, Dre was along for the ride.

We worked on the book for a couple of months before finishing. I soon designated my mom to be my editor, and my dad supplied printing paper he acquired from his job. The book's plot follows a young boy in a fictional home. The boy had continuous encounters with the supernatural world, in and out of his dreams. Although, his parents never believed his ghostly encounters. Out of frustration, the boy does whatever he can to prove them wrong, and what he see's, is real.

The book's concept was better as an idea than it was a book of any kind. My mom had a hard time editing the manuscript written by two fifth graders. She tried to re-write the text for us, but her efforts failed as she couldn't understand it. And my dad's ability to keep supplying our paper came to a halt a few hundred pages later.

Nonetheless, I continued with the single-copy production of my first book. I wanted my product to look and feel like a real book. Similar to the Goosebumps novels I grew to love. A softcover book with raised, emboiled, and colorful font on the front cover. I knew the book was incomplete and would never leave the confines of my home. But, at the least, I wanted something I could hold on to after all the time invested.

Using what was leftover from the printer paper, I made the cover and backing of the book. First, I glued a few stacks of paper together and trimmed them to size. Once they dried, the sheets hardened to the consistency, as hard as an actual, published book. Then, using markers and colored pencils, I designed the cover images and title of the book. To embroil the title's font, I used the back-end of a pencil to trace the opposite side of the font. Then, after leaving it out to dry for a few days, I carefully glued the pages inside. Finally, titled Gooselumps, the book was complete.

I never shared the book with anyone. In fact, it stayed on a shelf in my room until I moved out. The book exists to this day. Although, I haven't taken the time to read it since. It's stayed under the careful watch of my mom, stored in one of her old shoe boxes. Regardless of where my family decided to move, my Gooselumps book was there.

Time continued its steady tick, and I, for lack of better terms, grew up. I graduated high school, joined and deployed with the army, and wrote genres other than horror. But, every now and again, I'd think about the story Dre and I wrote from time to time and the fun I had writing it. However, I never gave the idea much thought to writing a fictional, scary story again.

The good times I had creating my semi-scary stories, although, are moments I'll cherish forever. Writing long hours with Dre, bouncing ideas off one another, and creating a world of our own. While the moments were brief, stepping away from reality, they were unforgettable. At night, while dreaming, I'd sometimes find myself exploring the Gooselumps world, Dre and I built.

It wasn't until two years ago, again, the idea to write another Goosebumps style book crossed my mind. The challenge of telling a scary story seemed complicated compared to the flawless execution of R.L Stine. I was admittedly hesitant at first and unsure if I should take another shot at it. But, the thought of giving it another attempt was too nostalgic.

Although, on this try, I would tell the story the best way I knew how. I didn't want to tell the story from the perspective of a fictional child with mythical stories. They say the easiest stories to articulate are often those that are true. So, I decided to use some of my own real-life experiences.

The stories that are told within the following chapters are mine. While some events are slightly altered, they are how I experienced and remember them. I hope you enjoy them.

WALKER DRIVE

Unknown at the time, our neighborhood was constructed on top of an old cemetery. A report later published around 1998 revealed that graves dated back as early as the 1800s.

DAY 0: (ENCOUNTER, 0)

They say home is where the heart is. My home was a kaleidoscope full of unforgettable childhood memories, with a heartbeat of its own. I grew up in a small community in Maryland, tucked-away on a small street named Walker Drive. My dad used to say, *"You can spit from the front door of the house, and it'll land in the back yard."*

After an assignment in Germany, my parents finally decided to move here for a few years. A cheap housing area until they could save enough money to buy a larger home with adequate living space. One with enough room for our four-person family. There was a military installation not too far from our new neighborhood. It was less than a thirty-minute commute for my dad, who worked on the base.

This was their first home together, after years of moving from one apartment to the next. But, while it was their first, it was anything far from bragging. The homes on Walker Drive were similar to townhomes. Two separate households conjoined at their sides made one housing unit. There were seven of these units, making fourteen families total, in my neighborhood.

They were narrowly spaced apart along an inverted cul de sac. The housing units faced outward from each other towards a road that encircled the community. There wasn't much of a view from the front lawns either. Two similar housing units were in front of our home, on the opposite side of the narrow street. Tall evergreen trees surrounded the area around the two and along the perimeter. As a kid, I never ventured too far into the wooded area. Thick shrubs, bushes, and fallen tree logs made the site not only dangerous but nearly impossible to traverse.

Because each home faced outward, there was open space behind us. In this area, while not much, the neighborhood kids usually played. It was a small patch of land that was hardly maintained. And its appearance rarely ever routinely managed. Heavy foot traffic in the area was all that was needed to keep the lawns trimmed appearance.

There were no differences in appearance from one house to the next. Each looked exactly the same as the one a few units down. All of them were militarily uniformed. As they should have been. During World War 1, Walker Drive once housed troops while they trained on the nearby base. More than four hundred thousand soldiers passed through this area. They used it as a training site for three infantry and training battalions and one depot brigade.

Our home was a fairly small one. A two-story, concrete, and brick structure that sat atop a basement. Two windows on the top section of the house. And two windows on the bottom, with the main entry door separating them. It is possible, the architect lacked imagination when designing the homes. However, it may have been seen as modern ingenuity at some point, far in the past.

The side of our home was bare. There weren't any windows to distinguish the first from second levels. The sidings were concrete slabs, layered with old, cracked bricks. Sometimes, the sections of walls fell off, exposing large, open areas on the sides of the home. And the back, just as plain and simple. No striking difference at all, as it was a carbon copy of the front of the house. Two windows on the top, and two on the bottom with our back door separating them.

Walking into our home, concrete tiles made up the ground-level floor. During the cold winter months, walking barefoot felt like you were walking on thin sheets of ice. There wasn't any distinguishable separation of rooms on the main floor either. Instead, the concrete tile seamlessly flowed from one room into the next. The interior walls were all of the same material and color. An off-white concrete that maintained a dingy appearance regardless of how often you cleaned them.

A space large enough to take off your

shoes as you entered was the foyer. And straight ahead, a few feet away, was our living room. This was the area my family spent time together and entertained ourselves. Although it was larger than the rest of the rooms in the home, the living room often doubled as a work area. And the room to the right of the living room was the dining room, which connected to our kitchen. From here, you could also access the back exit, leading to the playground.

A single flight of wooden stairs led from our living room to the second floor. The stairs were hardwood, made of solid oak. Judging by the noises and creeks they made walking up and down, they were as old as the house. And, on the second floor were three small bedrooms and the home's bathroom for the four of us.

My bedroom was on the backside of the house, just off the staircase as you reached the top. A room large enough to fit a few items. My bed and a toy chest my dad handmade. My bed faced the doorway and gave me a clear view of anyone coming up or down. To the right of my room was the bathroom. And, to the left was the hallway leading to my parents' and sisters' rooms. I was lucky enough to have one of the windows overlooking the playground behind me.

Furnishings were what you could expect from a young military couple starting off. The Items were relatively cheap and inexpensive. Most were gifts or hand-me-downs from friends and family who no longer desired to keep them. A well-worn, aged love seat and tabletop for the family living room older than I was. And entertainment set-ups from my parent's generation youth years. However, the German wall cabinet my parents brought with them added much-needed flavor to the interior of our home.

Then there's the basement of our home. You could access the underground room through a skinny wooden door in the kitchen. A flight of old wooden stairs led to the space below. I remember the staircase being rather small and narrow, sandwiched between thick concrete walls. A single exposed light bulb hanging from the ceiling was all there was to brighten the naturally dark room. It mainly served as a place to store away any unwanted items. I had little to no interest there and rarely made my way into the basement.

Next door to my family, in the conjoining house, were some of my best friends. Three siblings, military brats as myself, Keya, Tasha, and Erick. Their mom and dad both served in the army and were friends with my parents. Every now and again, both of our families would get together for outdoor cookouts and parties. And when their dad had to deploy during Desert Storm, my parents helped watch them.

My childhood memories, living on

Walker Drive, are as vivid as if they happened days ago. Although, today, the homes that once stood there are as if they were a place of fiction. And if you were to look it up on a map, there wouldn't be much to see. Some years later, before graduating high school, I decided to stop by the home I grew up in. A tall black metal fence now surrounded the community and blocked off its entrance. *DO NOT ENTER* was printed on vibrant white signs pinned to the surface of the fencing.

The roots of the Evergreen trees cracked the sidewalk. And unkept shrubs and weeds grew up through the asphalt of the street. The place had been abandoned for some time.

Most of the housing units on Walker Drive were crumbling to the ground, having been uncared for. And some, including where my home once stood, were completely gone. Only a small, square slab concrete where the front porch used to be, was all that remained.

And behind the homes, where the playground used to stand, resembled a dumping ground for discarded waste.

I wasn't sure what happened to my old neighborhood or why it was abandoned so quickly. It seemed as if the city thought it would be best to let it dissolve slowly into mother nature. The place was obviously forgotten and left to die. Communities continued to flourish in the surrounding area, and a new shopping center was built nearby. My neighborhood looked like life had been zapped out of it. Meanwhile, the surrounding areas sparked fresh, new life.

Who knows why our homes were left to rot. I asked a few friends who stayed close to the area if they knew anything but never received a definitive answer. Some said the costs of tearing it down were too expensive. Others thought it had something to do with a lack of interest from new, potential buyers. No one was for sure. However, I've wondered, did they abandon Walker Drive because of the strange and unexplainable events that sometimes occurred?

THE
WALKERS

Tales of the dead, returning from beyond the grave to visit us, have been told since ancient times. The spirits, souls, and the ghost of warriors, in particular. Some of the widely well-known come from the historic grounds of Gettysburg, Pennsylvania. For over one hundred years, there has been a myriad of reports involving the paranormal in the area.

On July 1, 1863, and on the fields of

Gettysburg, the Confederate and Union armies fought to their deaths. And, after three fierce days of fighting, nearly fifty thousand men lay dead. But, while the soldiers may have perished, that apparently didn't stop them from hanging around.

These stories reach far beyond the battlefields of the civil war. For example, a National Guard base in Missouri is also home to a few spooky accounts of ghostly apparitions. Today, reports of a soldier with a bullet hole through his head haunt the base's barracks. Legend has it, the ghost thinks he's still on duty during a raid. The soldiers living in the barracks also believe that the spirit sees them as the enemy.

***   ***

DAY 10: (ENCOUNTER, 1)

"Seven, eight, nine, ten!

Ready or not, here I come!" Tasha, my next-door neighbor, counted out loud.

The kids were playing a game of hide-n-seek just outside my bedroom window. But, it wouldn't take long to find who she was in search of. Tasha's brother and sister, Erick and Keya, hid behind slightly obscured obstacles in the small jungle gym. Unfortunately, there weren't many places to hide in our neighborhood. And there weren't many locations you could find that weren't used a thousand times before.

In Maryland, particularly during the warm summer months, hearing kids playing outside until sunset was normal. The electronic distractions today were mere dreams in the 80s and 90s. Instead, being outdoors, interacting, and sharing stories was our form of entertainment. Some of my fondest memories derive from a less technological era.

"Tag you're it!" Tasha screamed in excitement. Tagging her sister, who took an attempt at hiding behind a pair of inkberry shrubs.

"Come play hide-n-seek with us, Nick!" Keya shouted as she passed my window, running towards home base.

"In a little bit," I enthusiastically shouted from my bedroom window.

The truth was, I didn't want to go out and play. Less than twenty-four hours ago, I had one of the most traumatic experiences of my childhood. The only reason Keya could see me in my window was that I was made to be in my room. If my dad wasn't insisting that I stay in my room, I wouldn't have been in there.

I didn't do anything wrong, nor was I in

trouble taking a time out. Instead, my dad was teaching me how to overcome fear. My dad, an Army Sergent, had the belief that I should face what scared me the most. With my chest out and meeting my fears head-on. Although, last night's events made the task seem easier said than done.

The memories from that night have remained with me to this day. The hair on my arms and back of my neck stand on end whenever I mentally revisit that night. It's also the reason I continue to find it uncomfortable to sleep while lying on my back.

There wasn't anything during that day that made it unusual. The day was as the day before, and nothing stood out that would make it peculiar. It was like any other day of the week in my household. My parents were home from work, tending to household chores and getting me ready for bed. For dinner that night, my mom made some of her notorious spaghetti and tomato sauce. A delicious pasta simmered throughout the evening that put off a five-star, authentic, Italian aroma.

Later that night, shortly after dinner, my parents took me upstairs and tucked me into bed. And, as she has done since moving into the Walker Drive home, my mom recited a prayer over me. First, she would ask God to send angels to stand guard over me as I slept. Then, requesting each angel take up positions standing at the four corners of my bed frame.

"Goodnight, son. I love you." My dad said, slightly closing my bedroom door behind him as he walked out. However, he made sure not to close my door completely. Leaving a small enough space between the door and the frame, allowing the bathroom light to peek in.

"Goodnight, dad. I love you too." I responded as I snuggled tight into my sheets and blanket. Soon, closing my eyes and drifting off to sleep. Falling asleep for me as a kid was never an issue. Although, I can contribute some of that to the environment around me. Summer nights in my neighborhood and household were relatively quiet.

A few hours or so must have passed before suddenly being startled awake. Not by a loud bang, whispers, or the sounds of footsteps. Instead, silence. It was as if someone flipped a switch and shut off the sound. The kind of sound that you can always hear, no matter how quiet your surroundings. As if the only sound I could hear were the air molecules shaking and vibrating deep inside my ears.

A near deafening silence. And accompanying the muted atmosphere was a blistering chill. Much colder than the breeze from an air conditioner vent or draft on a summer night. This cold was at a near-numbing temperature. One that shot up from my feet and sharply to the top of my head. A chill so frigid, it sent a shockwave throughout my limbs.

Goosebumps scattered across the surface of my skin like an outbreak of chickenpox.

I looked out and over the foot of my bed, out towards the doorway. The light shining from the bathroom caused me to squint and briefly shut my eyes. The intensity seemed harsher than previous nights. It took a few seconds, clearing the haze from my eyes. Then, I noticed that the door to my room was no longer semi-shut. It was now swung open, and the bathroom's light now fully illuminating my room.

Gazing through with barely squinted eyes, confused, I noticed a movement in the hallway. A man soon came into my field of view. Shocked, I pulled the sheets over my head and began to panic. I tried convincing myself that indeed it was my dad. Probably, going to investigate the same cause that woke me from my sleep.

I failed miserably, trying to fool myself

otherwise. And, I knew any further attempts would be met with the same results. Only catching a brief glimpse of the man, I still knew it wasn't my dad. Instead, this was someone I had never seen before. There was something off about the man I had just seen in the hallway. Everything about his demeanor ensured me the man was not my dad.

I knew this was more than a case of my eyes playing tricks on me. The way he presented himself. His sense of urgency. Everything was off about him. However frightened, I decided to see if the man was still there. I slowly pulled the sheets from over my eyes and peered out into the hall. I was in disbelief at what I saw through the doorframe of my room. The sight, causing me to feel as if I had been punched in the stomach and lost my breath.

A man slowly walked the length of the hallway and passed my room. I could make him out to be around the same height as my dad. Around five foot ten inches, maybe an inch or two taller. He had come from the direction of my parent's bedroom to the left of mine. Walking at a steady pace from left to right. The man momentarily went from my view as he walked towards the bathroom. Only to become visible once again as he nonchalantly turned and drifted down the main flight of stairs.

"D...D..." I opened my mouth and attempted to call my dad. Except, as I tried, only a partial sound was produced. "D...D...Da..." Again, nothing.

It was the first time that I had ever been so terrified that I wasn't able to scream for help. As if the words I tried to produce became lodged in the center of my throat.

I continued watching the man walk down the stairs that led into the family room. The top of his head gradually disappeared behind the stairway as he walked down. With two bald fists, I rubbed my eyes as hard as possible. Trying to clear up the images my eyes were showing me. By now, the silence had lifted, and I could make out the ambient sounds inside my home. However, the bitter coldness remained. It was like a blanket of stagnant cold air lying over the top of me.

The more I focused, and as time elapsed, I better understood what was taking place. A cloud of mist, or sort of fog, had materialized outside my door. However, it wasn't the kind of fog I was used to seeing. Instead, its consistency was as if someone was standing in the hall, puffing and blowing cigar smoke. But, unlike cigar smoke, it didn't dissipate and evaporate over time.

A moment later, a second figure appeared. Just as the man before. Walking from the direction of my parent's room and passed the entrance to my room. But, only this time, I was able to make out some of his physical

features. A fairly young man. He had a fair-
skinned tone to his appearance. Who, I assumed
to be between the ages of twenty and twenty-
five.

As he walked, it was as if he were
floating. His stride was smooth and steady,
maintaining a perfect rhythm. Left foot, right
foot. Left. Right. And so on. He never once
looked in my direction. Keeping his head
straight ahead, unwavering as he walked. It was
as if his head were attached to a stick.

His attire seemed outdated. He wore a
drab olive top that appeared to be made of wool.
I remember comparing the fabric to the kind
that made my skin itch. The man also wore
matching slacks, with the areas around his
thighs puffed and poking outward. In addition
to his wardrobe, he sported an oddly shaped hat.
It had a rather large, circular brim that wrapped
all the way around it. And for his footwear, a
pair of old leather boots extending up past his

calves.

"*An army man?*" I thought to myself. Having parents that served in the army, I was accustomed to seeing uniforms.

I kept my gaze focused and looked out through my doorway. My sheets pulled up beneath my eyes. By now, the man had finally made his way down the stairs. Just as the first. I lay frozen in bed, lying on my back. Too scared to move as I waited, hoping the two men were gone for good. Unfortunately, I was wrong.

Wearing the same dingy, military-style uniform, a third man began walking past my room. Then another. And behind him, another. All of the men in similar clothing, appearance, and walking in unison with one another. A procession of men, all of which, appearing to be soldiers. In a final act of desperation, I pulled my covers up and over my head and eyes. Wishfully thinking everything I perceived as nothing more than a bad dream.

"*Protect me, protect me, protect me,*" I recited to myself, wishing my guardian angels would swiftly intervene.

Slowly, I wiggled the sheets from off over my eyes. Just enough so that I could see if the men were still there. Still, they remained. All of them, marching single file and continuing to disregard my existence. It was as if I no longer existed. Like I had slipped out of my world and woke up in an eery, new reality.

Left foot. Right foot. Left foot. Right foot. Pivot, left turn. Left. Right. The lockstep advancement of soldiers seemed neverending.

My perception of time slugged along at a snail's pace. Almost as if time itself had taken a break and stopped. What must have been a few minutes of elapsed time, to me, felt like hours. Then, without warning, the steady flow of soldiers looked as if it was coming to an end. One of the men abruptly stopped in the center of my door frame.

The soldier stood perfectly still and continued facing forward. The light from the bathroom fully illuminated his frontside. His eyes had a permanent, settled gaze in his eyes as he looked straight ahead. Never once blinking. And, the expression on his face gave me the impression of lifelessness.

In that instant, as if something called the soldier to attention, his body snapped and faced toward me. After a brief pause, he took an aggressive stride into the entrance of my doorway. The soldier maintained his dead, none expressive face as he made his way closer to me. His eyes shifted from straight ahead and now in my direction. Although, his gaze was not focused on me as I lay frozen in fear in bed. Instead, he appeared to be looking through and beyond my presence.

By now, the soldier made it to within a few feet from the foot of my bed. And, whatever fear that prevented me from screaming out for help suddenly lifted. Hurriedly, I pulled the blanket off from over me and sprung up out of my bed. Then, closing my eyes, I ran for my life as fast as I possibly could in the direction of my door.

"Daddy! Mommy!" I yelled at the top of my lungs.

As I made it into the hall, I quickly turned and ran into the bathroom. Jumping on top of the toilet seat, I curled myself up into the fetal position. Running in the opposite direction meant I would be heading in the path, the soldiers came.

"Nicholas!" I heard my dad's voice shouting from inside his bedroom. The fear in his voice was unmistakable. Within an instant, my dad had made his way to me.

"It wasn't me!" I screamed loudly, crying to my dad. I didn't want him thinking that it was me, walking through the house this entire time.

My dad dropped to one knee and held me tight, rocking me back and forth.

"I know, son. Mom and I saw it too." My dad went on to tell me that they both witnessed the same thing. I stayed in my parents' room for the remainder of that night. Getting back to sleep after the ordeal I encountered was nearly impossible.

The events from that night stayed with me throughout the years. In vivid detail, as if they happened nights ago. Regardless of how much my mom and dad strayed me away from talking about it. I've thought, on occasion, perhaps, it was my family's way of coping with what we saw. Or was it to shield and protect a fragile young mind. A mind from a dark realm of reality that they assuredly knew exists.

DAD'S CRY

For nearly eight thousand years, the Choctaw Indians have had an ancestral footprint in the southeastern region of the United States. Today, only four tribes of the Choctaws remain. Within Choctaw tribes, stories of the afterlife, spirits, and human-like creatures were widely told. One of these stories, in particular, was of Nalusa Falaya. Simply translated, it means, long black being.

According to the Choctaw story, the Nalusa Falaya often took on the form of a man. His eyes were extremely small, and his ears were said to have been long and pointy. The Nalusa Falaya was also known to sometimes slide on his belly rather than walking humanly upright. The Choctaw believed the shriveled-looking, shadowy figure to attack hunters and children at nightfall.

Those who crossed paths with Nalusa Falaya were bewitched with its dark magic. First, calling out to its victim to gain their attention. Then, those who fell for the shadow figures trick, looking at it, fell paralyzed to the ground. Once on the ground, Nalusa Falaya would insert a thorn or needle into its victim. According to the Choctaw, this caused the individual to commit terrible acts against others.

The victim would have no recollection of the encounter. They wouldn't be able to recall themselves being stuck with a thorn either. Only realizing after the evil acts were committed that it was Nalusa Falaya.

There's also Nalusa Chito. Sometimes

referred to as Impa Shilup, meaning *Shadow Creature*. Nalusa Chito, among the Choctaw, was said to have been a devourer of souls. The creature was tall, dark, and resembled that of a humanoid semi-shadow figure.

The Shadow Creature was known to have been called upon, or summoned, rather materializing out of thin air. Impa Shilup arose from the depths of an individual's darkest thoughts and depression. Once conjured, and in this reality, the shadow creature began eating on the soul that it dwelled in. Impa Shilup did not discriminate to whom the soul belonged. Men, women, children, young and old were all viable candidates.

Although, the tales of these otherwordly beings stretched far beyond the tribes of the Choctaw Indians. The history of these shadowy figures can be dated back as early as six hundred B.C.E. Moreover, they can be found in stories from all parts of the world, throughout various cultures. All with striking similarities.

A psychic medium, Natalia Kuna, is known for her encounters with these dark creatures. She also describes them in the same fashion as those long before her time. She accounts them as being tall, standing over seven feet in height. Their arms and legs were long as well. Rarely did she see them having any signs of hands or fingers.

While their names have changed over the years, shadow creatures continue to be spoken of today. Today, they are simply referred to as the Shadow People. A quick online search goes on to show how often people experience these paranormal beings. In fact, they've been made so popular, the fictional Slender Man was inspired by them. And in more recent years, films such as *Shadow People* and *Come True* depict terrifying tales of these notorious figures.

There are several opinions from

skeptics, phycologists, and paranormal investigators as to what Shadow People are. Some of the most popular include hallucinations and various forms of sleep paralysis. Other theories include substance abuse, sleep deprivation, or heightened emotional states. The exact reasoning behind the mysterious beings remains left unclear. However, the universal consensus is people are left feeling a sense of terror and dread when encountered.

*** ***

Day 185: (Encounter, 3)

I was raised by two hard-working parents. They did what they could to make ends meet. And both served in the military before moving on to their careers as civilians. After leaving the army, my mom had to work two and sometimes three jobs as our family got on its feet. My dad remained in the military for a few years after my mom completed her military contract. Although, after my dad's army retirement, he held jobs, including a UPS truck driver and a contractor for the government.

However unfortunate, it is common for military families to endure a brief struggle after leaving the service. Dedicating years of life to the military leaves little time for personal business and affairs. In the military, your time and what is conducted in that time are managed by the army. Job searching, resume building, and house hunting are time-consuming and require days, if not weeks and months. An important period that is desperately needed but rarely on the army's schedule.

Regardless of the hard times, my family encountered, I always saw my parents as real-life superheroes. My dad was as tough as nails. A Man of Steel, Superman himself. A bit too strict and disciplinary every now and again, but firm. A quiet man. When he spoke, he meant it. In stature, he was bigger than average. But, as someone who lifts weights and sometimes competed as a bodybuilder, he had to be.

And, standing five foot two inches tall, my mother gave only a love a mother could provide. Small country living, and as sweet as the peaches, from the state she was raised. Georgia. But I wouldn't take her southern heart for a weakness. Mom also wasn't the type of person to let anyone push her over either. In the army, she often outscored her male counterparts on physical tests. And, as a child, she had a reputation of being a brawler.

During the period in time, with my parents working multiple jobs, the environment was stressful. I always knew when my parents were going through financial hardships and struggles. Even as a young kid, I could sense frustration, worries, and tension in the atmosphere. Kids tend to pick up on these emotions extremely well. Especially when my parents tried concealing them from me. Regardless of how tough and strong their personalities were, I always knew.

I assume that's one of the many reasons this Saturday afternoon particularly stands out more than others. That was the first day my dad's emotional hardshell seemed to finally weaken and crack. My dad's approach to physical and emotional pain was to simply ignore it. It was rare for my dad to ever blow a gasket out of anger in front of me. Sure, he'd get pissed every so often, with the stresses of struggling to make ends meet. But my dad, at the least, kept his emotions out of sight.

Our home, on Walker Drive, had a total of three floors. All three were evenly spread across one thousand and two hundred square feet. Two floors of livable space and a basement. If my dad ever had the need to lash out or express his frustrations, he kept them away from our family. Rather than introduce the family to his frustrations, he went to the only room where he could be left alone. As well as try and disguise his obvious sounds of frustration.

The basement, the most unoccupied room in our home, was my dad's space. It's the area where he kept all of his weight lifting equipment and workout gear. Up above, hanging from exposed wooden beams in the ceiling, was his punching bag. An old army, canvas, duffle bag that he stuffed full of old clothes and blankets. And besides a few stacks of cardboard boxes along the wall, that's pretty much all the room could hold.

I could always tell how frustrated or worried my dad was, whether he hit the bag or not. If our financial situation started to look grim, the punching bag was the chosen outlet of release. Or, if he was having a bad day at one of his jobs, he'd lift weights. Over the years, I quickly grew to learn how my dad dealt with his emotions.

The sun shined brighter that day on a beautiful Saturday afternoon. My thighs were still burning. And, for some time, a large charlie horse had been trying to form in my calve. But, I could care less at that moment.

I was riding high on the adrenaline rush from earlier that day. The final game of my little league softball season, and our team took home the big win. I even had a few base hits and scored a point for the team. This was the first game that I was able to run across the home base. I felt like I was on top of the world.

After the game, the kids from the team went out to celebrate at a local pizza shop. However, my parents decided to have our post-game celebration at a location more in line with our financial situation.

I was seated comfortably at our four-person dining room table. My mom served me up a bowl of Frank-n-Beans, similar to pork and beans, but substitutes hot dogs for pork. Along with one of my mom's homemade butter bread biscuits, with a crunchy bag of my favorite corn chips. And to wash it all down, a ghostbusters-themed, green slime juice box.

After serving me, my mom made her way upstairs after deciding that she would take a shower. My dad, on the other hand, made his way off into the basement. His decision seemed out of place, considering how the day was going. Earlier that morning, my parents seemed excited about my last game of the season. They cheered for me throughout the game, and I'm fairly certain my mom was beginning to lose her voice. And, at one point, almost getting into an argument with the umpire over a bad call. But, the look of joy and pride in my parent's eyes was what was most impressionable.

The energy seemed to remain with us,

well after the game was over. I was under the impression that my parents were on the same emotional high as I was. The long grind of the hustle and bustle work week was over for them. It was rare either of them had a bad day when they had time off from work. That was especially true on Saturdays like today. I guess that's why my dad's basement visit is what struck me as odd.

Muffled thuds on the punching bag usually accompanied my dad shortly after closing the basement door behind him. If it wasn't his fists banging away on the bag, then heavy iron weights clanking against the concrete floor typically followed. But, despite that, today, there was silence. Sitting at the dining room table, I was unsure what to make of the calm. I knew after my dad had exerted his frustrations away, things tended to feel better at home.

After a few moments, I finally heard

something emitting from the basement floor. The sound was faint at first. It was hard to tell exactly what it was or if I had heard anything at all. And honestly, it wasn't the sound of something I had heard before in the basement.

Paying no mind to it initially, I brushed it off. Thinking that I heard things that, simply not worth my attention. By now, I was halfway through my meal. The adrenaline from the day's game was just starting to wear off. Then, I heard it again. Only this time, the sound lasts longer. While faint, the sounds of a whimpering man echoed up from the basement.

There are two events in my life that forever changed the superhero perspective I had of my dad. The first of the two instances was seeing him shed blood. My dad decided one morning that he would take me on a fishing trip at a local park. Just the two of us. Baiting one of the hooks on his fishing line, my dad pricked his finger. A red drop of blood slowly formed and pooled on the tip of his index finger.

My eyes widened in shock, watching him wipe it away on the leg of his pants. It was like I was watching Superman, being introduced to kryptonite for the first time.

"I'm okay, son. It's just a little scratch," He said in a calm, comforting tone. As if it were no big deal to him. But, there wasn't much he could do or say to lessen the concern I had for him. After seeing that he could bleed, I saw he was human, made of flesh. My dad could be hurt as much as I could.

The second occasion was today. Saturday afternoon sitting at the dining room table. After hearing my dad weep shocked me to the core, and I wasn't sure how to process it. Even more so than when I saw his finger bleeding. I wasn't sure if I should run and tell my mom or stay at the table and finish eating.

My dad's whimpering was strikingly out of his character. And not due to his strong and tough outer appearance. But, because it went against what my dad believed and instilled in me. *Take the pain, throw it away!* That was the philosophy on life that he often preached. He was especially adamant about it when it involved crying. So, if I'd fall and scrape my knee, crying was an option that was rarely available.

That doesn't mean, however, I sometimes forgot. Allowing a tear to fall as I went to my dad for comfort, I was promptly reminded. Grabbing my knee, or where the pain resided, my dad made me take it and throw it to the ground. Then, in a final act of ridding the pain from my body, I was made to step on it. Thus, destroying the pain once and for all, never allowing it to affect me again.

The cries from the basement continued. But now, they were loud enough to the point I could hear quivering in my father's voice. I almost removed myself from the table to tell my mom. But, thinking, the time it would have taken her to get out of the shower, I decided to stay.

My curiosity and concern for my dad, by now, had taken over. Getting up from the table, I walked over towards the door leading to the basement. Before I could reach out to turn its rusty-golden, metallic doorknob, the sobbing had stopped. *Did he hear me?* I remember thinking to myself. There weren't any sniffles or coughs that typically followed after crying.

Regardless, I continued to make my way down and check on my dad. The stairway and the room below were dimly lit. The lightbulb hanging near the bottom of the stairs hadn't been turned on either. *Odd?* My dad continued to remain silent as I cautiously crept down.

The basements stairs were old. A few of them, in the late stages of rotting and snapping in half. Made of thick planks of old plywood, they creaked loudly as you stepped on each one.

You had to be extra cautious about which floorboards you were going to step on. There was a good chance you could fall through.

Nearing the bottom stair, I stood on the tips of my toes. Reaching for the pull string on the bulb. But, before I could do so and turn on the light, I heard the cry again. This time, my dad's cry was more distinct. The crying appeared to be coming from the wall, near the corner of the room, to my left.

"Dad?" Worried, I called out to him.

While somewhat hard to see in the dim room, light from the kitchen provided some lighting. I left the door leading into the basement open, which allowed the light to shine through. I took a few steps towards the sound of my dad, neglecting to turn on the lightbulb. I knew there wasn't anything to fear as long as my dad was down there with me. I could care less if I saw my dad crying down there alone. I know he may have felt a sense of shame, allowing me to see him in such a vulnerable state. But, the love and respect I had for him would have remained the same.

Without a response from my dad, I continued, walking in the direction I heard him crying a short distance away. He continued to cry, stopping and starting back up again in short, periodic bursts.

"Dad, are you okay? Mom's upstairs in the shower." I knew that he knew where my mom was. But I didn't know what else to say.

Informing my dad of my mom's whereabouts was simply the first thing that came to my mind. And again, my calls to my dad went unanswered. Although, by now, I could see him. His crying has also seemed to have stopped.

I stood a few paces away, making sure not to get too close. My dad was crouched down behind a column of four cardboard boxes stacked one on top of the other. As he faced the wall, I could make out the outermost portion of his back, right side. The room was completely silent. No more crying, no more whimpering, no more sounds of sorrow. Nothing. Not even the sound of the old water heater, which sometimes made strange popping noises.

The silhouette of my dad just sat there, motionless. It reminded me of how I act when my parents catch me being mischievous. I then, for a third attempt, called out to my dad. And, at that instance, the figure behind the stacked boxes abruptly stood upright.

A tightly balled-up figure slowly rose up, allowing me to get a better view of him. I soon noticed how tall the figure was, and I was instantaneously stricken with fear. For a brief moment, I wondered how something so large appeared as small as it did behind the boxes. It reminded me of how a Footlong Fruit Roll-Up candy, unrolled as you pulled it from the wrapper. Or like a coiled snake would unravel before striking. Only instead of unleashing a lethal bite, erecting itself to stand on its tail end.

The figure was as solid dark as the pits of the corner from which it came. Some aspects of it were that of a shadow. Except, it had the characteristics of a being with physical mass and properties. While, in other ways, managed to resemble nothing more than a black void in space.

The shadow figure towered over the cardboard boxes and stood silently, at what seemed a few feet away. The top of the shadow figure's head touched the top of the ceiling and extended into the wooden beams. Judging by the height of the basement ceiling, he must have stood seven or eight feet tall. His body appeared extremely frail and skinny, like a twig cut from the branch of a tree. There weren't any distinguishable arms or legs that I could make out. Only the tall, slender shadow of what I assumed to be that of a man.

With a stiffened posture, the tall shadow casually and deliberately leaned out from behind the boxes. Meanwhile, keeping the lower portion of its body hidden from view. Without a sound, the figure then extended its body even further skyward. Stretching its long figure until its head no longer had any room to travel. Finally, causing the shadow to bend at a ninety-degree angle where its shoulders met its neck.

I had no interest in sticking around to see what the unearthly figure would do next. Panic-stricken, I turned around and ran back towards the stairway. I remember holding my breath as I ran, unable to make a shout or scream for help. Luckily, I wouldn't have to. Before I could reach the top of the stairs, I saw my dad standing in the doorway. He carried a look of confusion and worry on his face.

"Hey! What's going on!" My dad's trembling voice called out, asking. "I heard you calling me. I was outside about to wash the car. Are you okay? What are you doing in there anyway? I thought you were supposed to be eating." He continued.

All I could do at the moment was hold onto my dad. Rather than try and explain to my dad what I saw or why I went into the basement. Honestly, I didn't think my dad would have believed me, even if I told him. So, I kept what I saw and experienced to myself. I felt that it would be best to never discuss the paranormal event with anyone. Especially my dad. Revisiting the sounds of my dad crying like a child was challenging to acknowledge. It would mean I had to tear down his hard exterior and expose a softer side I wasn't used to.

Although, I never saw the shadow figure again since that day in the basement. I didn't go out of my way to see if he were still there either. On the contrary, I made sure to take whatever actions I needed, to stay away as much as possible. But that doesn't mean the thought of the shadow man ever left my mind. I was curious if anyone else had seen the dark entity in our basement below. And, if so, effortlessly brushed it off. Not because they assumed it to be a figment of their imagination. Instead, because it's the simplest way to cope with what they undoubtedly witnessed.

playdate

Nearly five out of ten

American's, believe that demons, ghosts, and otherworldly spirits exist. If you, yourself, have also experienced the paranormal, then welcome to the club. These experiences aren't solely reserved for your average, everyday citizen. Some of the world's most prominent individuals have found themselves stepping into this unseen world as well. They were also widely vocal about their paranormal experiences.

One well-known figure, who's had his brush with spirits, was nonother than Winston Churchill. On a trip to the white house during WW2, the British prime minister witnessed a ghostly apparition. Wearing nothing but the skin on his body and a cigar after an evening bath, Churchill spotted the spirit of President Lincoln.

"Good evening Mr. President. You seem to have me at a disadvantage," Churchill reportedly said.

Harry Truman, America's thirty-third President, was someone else who's had an experience with the paranormal. His account of the ordeal is also documented at the presidential library and museum. While Truman doesn't speak of seeing apparitions, he does acknowledge noises he heard caused without explanation.

In a letter to his wife, Truman describes

being startled awake after hearing banging on his door, writing, "I went out and looked up and down the hall, looked in your room and Margie's. Still no one." The President went on further, writing in his letter, "There were footsteps in your room whose door I'd left open. Jumped and looked, and no one there! The damned place is haunted sure as shootin'."

DAY 97: (ENCOUNTER, 2)

My youngest sister, three years old at the time, and I hadn't seen my half-sister, Tatiana, in years. The last time Tatiana and I were together was on our family trip to Alabama, on a brief visit. Finally, we were all living under the same roof together. I guess things back at her home, with her mother, weren't working out. I knew she had a tendency to get into trouble in her sixth-grade class periodically. Maybe, it may have had something to do with a transfer of schooling systems? Or, perhaps disciplinary actions were lacking in her household? But, regardless of her past, I didn't care why Tatiana moved in with us. It felt good to have an older sibling around.

Tatiana had a relatively rough upbringing living with her mom. You know, the stories we're all too familiar with. A child raised in poverty, harsh environments at times, and under the care of a single parent. From the stories I heard as a kid, Tatiana was often bullied in grade school. However, over time and after years of being on the receiving end, she decided enough was enough. She hasn't been the same after taking a stand for herself and beating up the schoolyard bully.

In some ways, she became more outspoken and toed the line of rebellion. As a result, Tatiana constantly received less than stellar reports from her teachers and principal. Suspensions and expulsions from school were becoming more frequent. Tatiana would insist on going out swinging than being taken lightly or as a pushover. Unfortunately, her new personality and who she became caused her and her mother to clash.

After a few years of bad behavior, Tatiana's mother had finally had enough. Between my family and her mom, they agreed that a change of environment would be best for her. Maybe the parenting style or the kids she grew up with needed to change.

After my half-sister moved in under our roof, it wasn't long before she would fit right in. Within the first few months, she took care of and had her own set of chores and responsibilities. And, after school, she would look out for my younger sister and me while my parents were at work. Sure, there were a few occasions when Tatiana had difficulty getting accustomed to my family's rules. But, I assume that would be the case for just about anyone in a new environment.

Within the first few weeks of living on Walker Drive, Tatiana made a few close friends. Seeing her playing outside with her new mates seemed as if she had lived there her entire life. And considering her issues with making friends where she used to live, it felt good to see. Some of my best friends became her friends. In fact, most of the kids my age looked up to her as if she was their big sister.

Tatiana, in many ways, because of who she became, gravitated towards that role. A big sister and protector of sorts. Someone who had no problem watching out for the little guys.

However, she was attracted to two friends in particular. Two girls, older than I was and around Tatiana's age. I hadn't seen them before she moved in with us. The few occasions

I did see them were from a distance away. Usually, while playing with friends of my own, I saw the three of them hanging out with one another.

I assumed they lived close by or within walking distance, looking to make friends. However, whenever I did see them, they made sure to keep their limits to the area surrounding the playground. The two girls never utilized the jungle gym or swing set. And, there isn't a moment I can recall that I saw them play with the other kids. Only Tatiana.

The perimeter of the playground, behind our homes, was surrounded by woods and thick undergrowth vegetation. An area you were more likely to get eaten alive by bugs than you were to have a good time. The two girls would talk to Tatiana from the treeline, only to quickly leave and return to where they had come from. They would always show up sporadically. One day here, one day there. A few weeks or so would pass, and the girls would stop by again.

I never asked Tatiana who the girls were or where they lived. They were older than I was, so I thought that was why they didn't play with the rest of the kids. But, that all changed one day. It was the first and last time that I would see her friends again. That was also the first day Tatiana showed a fit of anger towards me. A rage I didn't think she was capable of.

The clock's hands, hanging from the living room wall, no longer ticked or moved. My parents hadn't changed the batteries in some time. I assume it was around two o'clock or so, judging from when I usually made it home after daycare. And, my younger sister was inside taking one of her daily naps. Tatiana had the duties of babysitting my younger sister and me until my mom made it home a few hours later. My mom was working two jobs at the time. While my dad juggled being in the army and a truck driver for UPS.

It was a beautiful North East summer afternoon. The weather was perfect for playing outdoors. Not a cloud in the sky. The temperature was a mild seventy-five degrees. It reminded me of the San Franciso weather depicted in movies. An occasional breeze that provided the perfect draft. The one that's not too chill or harsh.

On this day, regardless of the weather, I decided to stay indoors. Most of the kids enjoyed the day, riding bikes and playing on the playground and jungle gym. Granted, I did have permission to go out and play while my parents were away. Provided that I agreed to one of their stipulations. That I stayed within eyesight of my home and Tatiana.

My play area for the day was in the confines of my room. And, a Tyco Challenge One Hundred provided me more than enough entertainment than I needed. An electric, battery-operated two-car racing track. The cars ran on electric slots that supplied power to the car's electric motors. Using a handheld controller, you could increase the amount of voltage the track put out.

Tatiana, on the other hand, took the opposite approach and played in the nice weather. Sitting on the front steps in front of our house, enjoying the fresh air. She'd pop her head inside from time to time, checking on my sister and me. And while sitting in my room, I could hear the door open and close as she checked in on us. On days like today, the front door of our home was left unclosed, allowing a cool draft in.

We had one of the screen doors that operated on a metal spring hinge. If you didn't ease it closed, the spring caused the door to slam shut. I heard Tatiana as she ran inside and up the flight of stairs. Although my door was slightly ajar, I caught a glimpse of her sprinting past my doorway through the corner of my eye.

She sounded as if she was having a good time. Laughing and giggling out loud as she went by.

I continued listening until the sounds of her footsteps led into her room. Initially, I ignored her, thinking she was coming in to grab a toy. Tatiana's footsteps loitered. Tapping and sliding against the floor, from one side of her room to the next. Too much noise while our younger sister slept. I remember thinking she may wake her with all the commotion.

A few minutes passed, and Tatiana still lingered inside her room. Our rooms weren't large or spacious by any means. Her room had a bed and a small dresser. She brought the toys she could with her in a small box, now sitting on the side of her bed. And from what I could see in the box, there wasn't much of anything. A few dolls, a small playhouse, makeup kits, and other random toys were scattered throughout.

Then, all of a sudden, the noises from

Tatiana's room had stopped. I thought she finally found what she was looking for and was heading back out to play.

"Of course not. We can stay here." Tatiana jokingly said out loud.

For a moment, I thought she was talking to me. Although, I wasn't sure. I dialed back the knob on my race car controller and brought it to a stop. I didn't want the electric hum of the track interfering with what she was saying.

"Tati?" I calmly called out to her. Not loud enough to wake my sister, but loud so that she would hear.

Not receiving a response, I walked over to my door to take a peak out. Then, I heard Tatiana again. Or, at least it sounded like her. It was as if someone else was in the room with her, talking just underneath Tatiana's voice. A voice that I was unfamiliar with. I could distinguish my half-sister, but I could also hear another. The tone in which the other person spoke made it hard to determine what they were saying.

By now, I stepped out to investigate what I was hearing. Although I didn't see anyone behind Tatiana as she came in, I heard multiple whispers coming from inside her room. Any company, while my parents were away, was entirely against the rules. And, I feared for her and the repercussions if she were caught. We were somewhat of Tatiana's last bit of hope. Breaking these rules could result in her moving back in with her mom.

"Oh, thank you!" The voice of a girl whispered in a playful, joyful tone.

Who is that? I remember thinking. Having lived on Walker Drive for a few years now, I knew every kid's voice by heart. Besides, there were only four girls that lived in my neighborhood. Keya and Tasha, my next-door neighbors and best friends. And two older girls. Much older than Tatiana, Sarah, and Yasi, who lived down the street a few units away.

Making sure to watch my footing, I walked closer to Tatiana's room. I didn't want to cause the old wooden floorboards to squeak as I made my way down the hall. From a few feet away, I could see that her door was slightly left open. Looking through the narrow space, I saw Tatiana seated on the floor, legs crossed in front of her. She was playing with one of her dolls and combing its hair.

"Oh, hush it!" A faint yet aggressive voice breathed from inside the room. But, unfortunately, who the voice belonged to was out of my direct line of sight. The positioning of the door and its frame made it impossible to see.

Tatiana's eyes looked up at whoever was talking to her. Then, slowly, placed her doll down on the floor and slid it out in front of her. I took a couple of steps closer, getting a better view and seeing who she was playing with. Even if Tatiana had company over, I wouldn't have told on her. We were getting along great together, and I didn't want to see her have to leave.

I took a couple of steps closer to her door and leaned closer towards the door. But, unfortunately, I must have underestimated my balancing skills as I edged forward. In the act of managing not to fall, my hand slid against the door, causing it to slightly open. There was a moment of motionlessness as I stood there, looking into Tatiana's room. What I saw nearly caused my bottom jaw to hit the hard floor beneath me.

Startled, Tatiana's eyes abruptly shifted over in my direction. It was as if she had seen a ghost peaking into her room. Her hands tucked into her chest as she curled up her legs and tucked her knees into her chest. I never saw Tatiana, let alone anyone, in her state of shock and surprise. However, what I saw, shocked me just as much.

Two girls, sitting on the floor, perfectly still and unbothered. Both, in the same position. Sitting on the floor. Legs crossed at the ankles and facing towards Tatiana. Both appeared to be wearing identical outfits. Matching off-white, dingy, and stain-covered nightgowns that draped their legs as they sat. The two girls had long, brunette hair down to their lower backs. Neither of the two, bothering to look in my direction as I stared in.

Around the two girls was a sort of haze that engulfed them. The best I can describe it is as being a cloud of fog or mist. The mist surrounded them and had a shimmering effect. Flickering in and out of focus, like a lightbulb in its last dying seconds. The strange materialization made their appearances, at times, hard to focus on. It was as if they were slightly out of focus while the space around them, including Tatiana, was unbothered.

Then, one of the young girls sitting

closest to the door looked over in my direction. Her hair was pulled back and tucked over her right ear. She then paused, looking at me from her periphery. Her gaze was empty and now halfway fixed on me. I could barely make out any of her facial features. Although, I was able to see the dirt and dried mud that covered her pale jawline.

"*I know these girls.*" I thought silently. These were the same girls that I'd seen Tatiana talking to at the playground.

But, as quick as I was to make the connection to who they were, the two girls simultaneously vanished. Without blinking, and my eyes fixated on the two strange figures, I watched them disappear.

"Leave us alone! Go away, you little snot!" Tatiana yelled and hurled the doll she had been playing with at me. I thought she was going to kill me.

Tatiana jumped to her feet and ran

towards me, waving her fist above her head. All I could muster at first was to stand there paralyzed, numb, and confused. She had a sincere look of anger in her eyes as she ran towards me. But, instead of taking her rage against me, she slammed the door in my face. Shutting it with such a force that it caused the walls to shake. Not caring if the door would hit me or not. And furthermore, waking up our little sister from her nap.

I ran back to my room as fast as I could. Seeing an apparition was something I'd experienced in the past. But, up until that point, it was always an individual experience. This, however, was the first time I knew someone else had witnessed these paranormal beings.

After a few minutes of Jasmine's crying, Tatiana tended to her. I decided to stay in my room until my parents made it home, about an hour later. Tatiana and I never discussed the experience we had together that day. Instead, she seemed to have brushed it off as if nothing had happened.

I never saw the two girls again. Tatiana stopped wandering off towards the woods as well. It was almost like she knew that the two girls were no longer coming back. Or, perhaps, the three did continue seeing each other. It's the rest of us that no longer saw them.

(Heading off on my first day of school.)

(Start of the new school year, circa 1989.)

(Demonstrating a roundhouse kick on Walker Drive.)

(Me being an irritating big brother.)

(Focused during our Championship game!)

(My kindergarten photo while living on Walker
    Drive.)

(Softball Champions.)

(Grade school photo.)

(Circa 1987.)

(My youngest sister and I, in front of our home on Walker Drive.)

THE
BOARD

In the twenty-first century,

it's commonly agreed that there is life after we
die. At least, that's according to a poll
conducted in 2015 regarding the afterlife. This
study found that almost half felt that they had
seen the presence of a ghost. And, an even more

significant amount believed that they heard the voice of a passed loved one.

On its surface, to some, these unworldly claims may seem a bit far-fetched. However, science may provide the missing link between our reality and the afterlife. Within science, there are governing laws that remain unbreakable. Specific laws such as Newton's laws of motion and his laws of universal gravitation. Or Kepler's laws of planetary motion, describing the orbits of the planets around the sun. And my favorite, the laws of conservation of energy (LCE).

What is known today as, The First Law of thermodynamics, LCE states that energy is neither created nor destroyed. Instead, energy may only be transferred from one form to another. Suppose we were to take this law and somehow mesh it with the possibilities of the supernatural. In that case, we give birth to the afterlife. Thus, the lifeforce, or energy, that exists inside us all would not cease to exist after our life has ended. Instead, that energy is transferred from this reality to the next.

The human spirit has yet to be seen by the eyes of scientists. However, that doesn't mean they haven't investigated this mystical energy. For thousands of years, humans have spoken of and documented their beliefs of the existence of the human spirit. According to Platonists, those who study the philosophies of Plato, the soul is likened to that of the gods. An immaterial, formless, and unseen substance. The very essence of a human being.

According to others, it's twenty-one grams. That's the total weight of the human soul, according to one study. Duncan MacDougall, a doctor, living in Massachusetts during the 1900s, once carried out abnormal procedures determining just that. First, the doctor made a bed fitted with sensitive scales attached to it. MacDougall would then convince terminally ill patients to lie on the unique bed during their final moments.

At the exact moment of the patients' death, Duncan made a shocking discovery. There was a consistent weight reduction of twenty-one grams. This was after accounting for bodily fluids and gases like oxygen and nitrogen. While others within the scientific community rejected the doctors' work, Doctor MacDougall conducted the test on six occasions. His work, since his findings, has yet to be repeated.

***　　***

DAY 179: (ENCOUNTER, 4)

A chilly night tonight. The kind of chill that lets you know a cold winter was right around the corner. It was noticeably, however, colder this October than in recent years on Walker Drive. A possible foretelling of the blizzard that was soon to hit our state later that same year.

By now, most of the leaves had fallen from the trees. Decorated pumpkins littered front porches and spooky decorations scattered across front lawns. The kids next door were already showing off their costumes. Wearing them out during the day to play in. And I had the mouth-watering laundry list of candy that I wanted to have that year. Holloween was right around the corner.

My family was never into the Holloween traditions growing up. I've always assumed it to be because of my parents' religious background. But, for one reason or another, this year would be different. My parents decided to take part in this year's Halloween festivities. It felt great finally getting a chance to get out for a night of trick or treating.

My parents, weeks ago, bought my sister and I's costumes and prepped them early so we wouldn't miss out. My dad's costume took the longest to prepare of them all. His was a plaster mold of his face, designed to make him look like a demon. Once the mold hardened, he filled it with a plastic gel that would later become the mask. It was painted dark red and black, with long, devilish horns attached to the skull. I remember how frightened I used to get, seeing it. My mom was going to be a green, wicked witch this Halloween. I would go as a ninja warrior, inspired by old Bruce Lee films. And, my sister, a ballerina for this year's Holloween.

As a family, we carved out pumpkin designs as a competition to see who was the best. But, of course, my dad's artistry was always superior. We weren't used to the traditions of Holloween. But we had fun making them up as we went along. We didn't have family that lived nearby or could visit during the holidays. Being, my cousins, aunts, and uncles lived hundreds of miles away throughout multiple states.

We typically saw family during summer school breaks. But even those trips were limited. They were dependant on whether or not my parents were able to afford the financial hit. So, instead, the closest relatives I had growing up were my godparents. During my parents' time in the army, their friends became our family.

My favorite, non-biological family member of them all was Ms. Mandy. A close friend of my mom, Mandy, served the roles of godmother and auntie. One of my fondest memories of her was always keeping a stash of caramel chocolates in her purse. She'd sneak them to me behind my parents' back whenever she'd stop by.

My parents invited her over later that

night. Soon after, my sister and I went off to bed. They wanted to start a yearly tradition the week or so before every Halloween. Having the adults altogether, watching scary movies, and playing board games.

Falling asleep was harder than usual for some reason that night. It may be due to the commotion they were making in the downstairs living room. In our small home, the sound had the tendency to bounce and reverberate inside. I recall hearing my auntie stepping in that night. She and my mom greeted each other the way they always have. Both hugging each other around the neck, jumping up and down from side to side. And hearing the bottom of her shoes tapping against the concrete living room floor.

What seemed like a couple of hours went by, and I was still awake. Although, I did manage to drift off for a brief moment. That was until I heard my dad's heavy footsteps walking up the stairs in front of my room. I guess he thought we were sound asleep, and he wasn't going to disturb us. Normally, he was cautious of making noise on the stairs. For example, avoiding one of the uneven, cracked boards. In this case, however, he walked on each one.

I listened to him as he walked down the hall and into his room. I closed my eyes, pretending to sleep in case he decided to peek into my room. Although I wouldn't have to pretend long, as he was in his room for a short moment. It was enough time for him to grab something from his closet before heading back downstairs. I didn't know it at the time, but my dad retrieved an old Ouiji board.

My dad purchased the board game while stationed overseas in Germany. A 1972, Mystifying Oracle William Fuld Talking Board Set. The Ouiji board. I'd never seen it other than that night. A flat wooden panel with two semi-circles with the alphabet letters arranged at the top. The numbers zero through nine formed a line beneath the letters. *Yes* and *No*, at the top upper corners. And, *Goodbye*, at the bottom of the board. With the Ouiji also came a planchette. A special teardrop-shaped tool with a glass window at its center.

According to the instructions of the board game, two or more people were to sit around the board. Then, each individual places their fingertips on the planchette, asks a question, and waits and watches as the planchette moves from letter to letter. Looking through the glass window of the tool, highlighted a letter or number.

Once you've obtained the letters and numbers, you're then able to make out the answer. According to the story behind the game, the game's makers asked the board what they should call it before releasing it. The board replied and spelled out O U I J A. When asked

what it meant, the game replied, "*Good Luck*."
During the New age movement of the1970's
and '80s, the Ouiji board popularity increased.
The game's huge claim was that it could
connect the living with the dead. Although, it
was marketed as a form of family
entertainment.

Listening in on my family, I heard them
as they slid small furniture around to clear space
for the game. By now, the television and the
lights downstairs were turned off. Only the light
from the upstairs bathroom provided lighting in
the house.

"Hold on a second. I'll grab my
flashlight and tape recorder." My dad whispered
to my auntie and mom.

Keeping their voices barely loud enough
to be heard, they began playing the game. My
dad initiated the first question.

"Is there anyone here with us tonight?"
He hesitantly asked the board. No response. A

few moments passed before repeating the question. And again, silence.

While the adults remained preoccupied with the game, I took the opportunity to see what was going on. Quietly, I got up from my bed and crept towards the top of the stairs just outside my door. Then, remaining as still as possible, I leaned against the wall and peeked down into the living room. After countless trials and errors, I learned the best vantage point to see below without drawing attention.

The room was dark, and it was hard to make out everything in the room. Only my dad's flashlight dimly lit the area. He propped the light up so that it would shine over them as they played. My parents and auntie sat on the floor in a circular formation. In the center of them laid the Ouiji board. And next to the board was the tape recorder.

"This is crazy!" My aunt apprehensively stated. Making it known that she was uncomfortable about participating in possibly talking with the dead.

"Quiet, or you'll ruin the game." My dad interrupted. "Now, you ask a question, Sarah." He continued talking, this time to my mother.

I remained standing at the top of the stairs. Keeping as quiet as a mouse, looking and listening as closely as I could. My parents and Mandy held their fingers on the planchette, moving it on the board in a circular motion.

"If there is anyone here, can you give us a name?" My mom began to ask.

Then, after a moment of silence, the planchette began moving. It looked as if the small tear-shaped object slid on ice as it moved across the board's surface. Unfortunately, I couldn't make out where the device stopped or what it spelled out before it came to a sudden stop. My aunt snatched her hands away.

"You can't do that! We have to close out the game!" My dad said, taking note of one of the rules of the game.

"Well, let's hurry. I don't like playing this game anymore." She responded.

To end the paranormal session, the group must first say *Thank You* and *Goodbye* on the board using the planchette. If the group's circle is broken before doing so, it may result in bad luck or an unhappy spirit.

After properly closing out their Ouiji session, my dad grabbed his tape recorder and rewound it. He was in hopes that they would be able to hear the voice of a spirit. Having a tape recorder next to the Ouiji board and recording was said to enhance the experience. It's theorized that audio from the spirit world could be captured on the device. Inaudible without the aid of a recording device, these recordings are known as electronic voice phenomena (EVP).

The three of them sat and listened quietly as the recorder played. At first, it was what you would have expected. I could hear my dad asking questions, followed by the room's ambient noise in the background. The sliding of the planchette on the board. And so on. The recorder appeared in good condition and operating properly.

However, the recorder's functionality took an abrupt turn as the tape played on further. Towards the end of the recording, when my mom poses her question, a static popping sound begins playing in the background. The kind of interference you hear when changing stations on a dial radio. The sound grew louder and popped rapidly. Soon, it became so overwhelming, my dad attempted shutting it off.

Everyone initially thought the recorder needed new batteries or possibly malfunctioning. Before my dad could stop the tape and grab a fresh pair of batteries, the recording played a loud, high-pitched squeal. Loud enough to make my mom and aunt flinch and take hold of one another's hand. My dad froze in place and was now standing in front of the Ouji board.

A few moments later, the ear-piercing squeal became more perceptible. Over the small tape recorders speaker, the distinct sound of a car's screeching tires sliding over asphalt played. As if a car were traveling at great speeds before fully applying and locking the breaks. All the while swerving, trying to regain control of a runaway vehicle. A bone-crushing blast, one that's typical with a car accident, then followed.

"I love you.." A delicate voice said on the recording. It was like one last, final message. The recorder abruptly stopped and completely shut down after that.

My parents and Mandy looked as if they were glued motionless in time. And myself, just as inanimate. Unsure as to what we all heard and experienced.

"*BANG*!" A loud thud resonated from the house. It, at first, sounded like it came from inside the walls of the living room. As if the home was hit violently with something of substantial size. My dad tossed the tape recorder instantaneously onto the living room sofa.

The thud was strong enough that it caused our living room Shrunk to rattle and vibrate. A large, German piece of furniture made of solid oak with glass fixtures. Like an oversized cabinet, the Shrunk is where the family television and other decorative items were held. However, far from a delicate or lightweight piece of furniture. Our Shrunk weighed a few hundred pounds and took a team of four men to lift.

Terrified, I ran back into my room, in my bed, and covered my face with my bedsheets.

"I can't! I'm leaving!" My aunt said, soon closing the front door behind her.

Laying in bed, I tried to listen in on what

my parents were going to say. I hoped they would have a reasonable explanation as to what happened. However, my clarification never came after I eventually fell asleep. The last I remember from that night was my dad bringing the Ouiji board back into his room.

My Aunt Mandy managed to make it back the following week and go trick or treating with us. Although, she never brought up the events of that night. My parents and Mandy carried on as if nothing abnormal had occurred. I didn't dare to ask any questions at that time. Especially when I was supposed to be asleep the night it happened. Asking questions was a self admittance to breaking mom and dad's rules.

It would take decades before finally deciding to pose the question as to what happened that night. It was shortly after my high school graduation, right before enlisting into the army. My parents, who as well, recall the night vividly and with great detail.

"That voice that came through on the recorder was your aunts' older sister." My mom went on to say. "She rarely ever talked about it with anyone. Only those who were close to her, like family."

My mother went further into detail about Aunt Mandy's sister. While my aunt was still a teenager, her sister was involved in a fatal car accident. One night, after leaving her job, my aunt's sister lost control of the wheel due to uncertain circumstances. My aunt never saw photos of her sister's accident. So it was also understandable that she had a rough time accepting her sister's passing.

My aunt wanted to know, over time, if her sister felt pain or passed immediately. It was also her wish to know that if her sister had any last words before her passing, what they were. Finally, the night of my parents' Ouiji board session, they believe she received the answer to her wish. The voice on the recording, according to my aunt, was indeed her sister. All three recall the voice saying, "*I love you*…," before the recording stopped

ABOUT THE AUTHOR

NICHOLAS IRVING is the *New York Times* bestselling author of *The Reaper* and *Way of the Reaper*, and his novel series, including Reaper Ghost Tartger, Reaper Threat Zero, and Reaper Drone Strike.